"Hi, Pizza Man!"

by VIRGINIA WALTER

pictures by PONDER GOEMBEL

Orchard Books • New York

"Mama!"

"I know you're hungry, Vivian.
It's so hard to wait
for the pizza man to come.
He'll be here soon."

"What will you say when the doorbell rings and we open the door?"

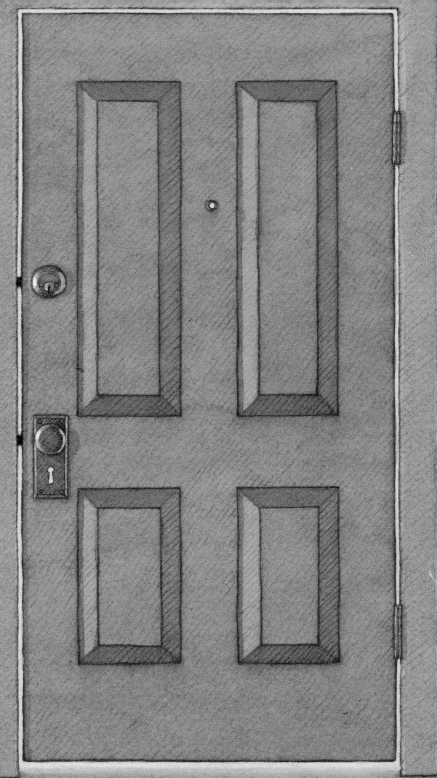

"Hi, PIZZA MAN!"

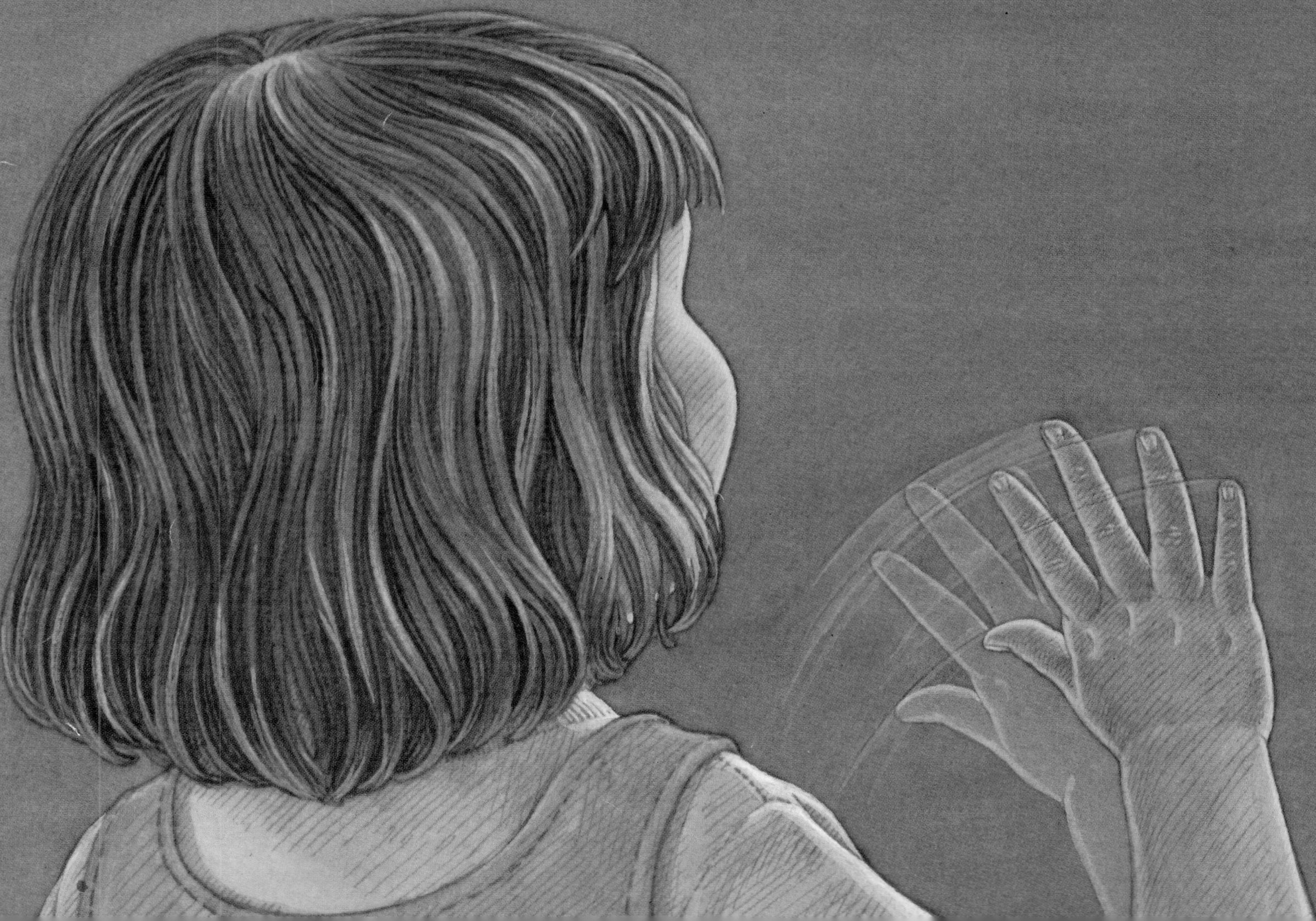

"What if it's not a pizza man?
What if it's a pizza woman?
Then what will you say?"

"HI, PIZZA WOMAN!"

"What if it's not a pizza woman? What if it's a pizza kitty?
Then what will you say?"

"MEOW MEOW, PiZZA KiTTY!"

"What if it's a pizza dog? Then what will you say?"

"WOOF WOOF, PIZZA DOG!"

"What if it's a pizza duck? Then what will you say?"

"QUACK QUACK, PIZZA DUCK!"

"What if it's a pizza cow? Then what will you say?"

"MOOO O O O, PIZZA COW!"

"What if it's a pizza snake? Then what will you say?"

SSSSSS, PIZZA SNAKE!"

"What if it's a pizza dinosaur? Then what will you say?"

"ROAR, PIZZA DINOSAUR!"

RING! RING!

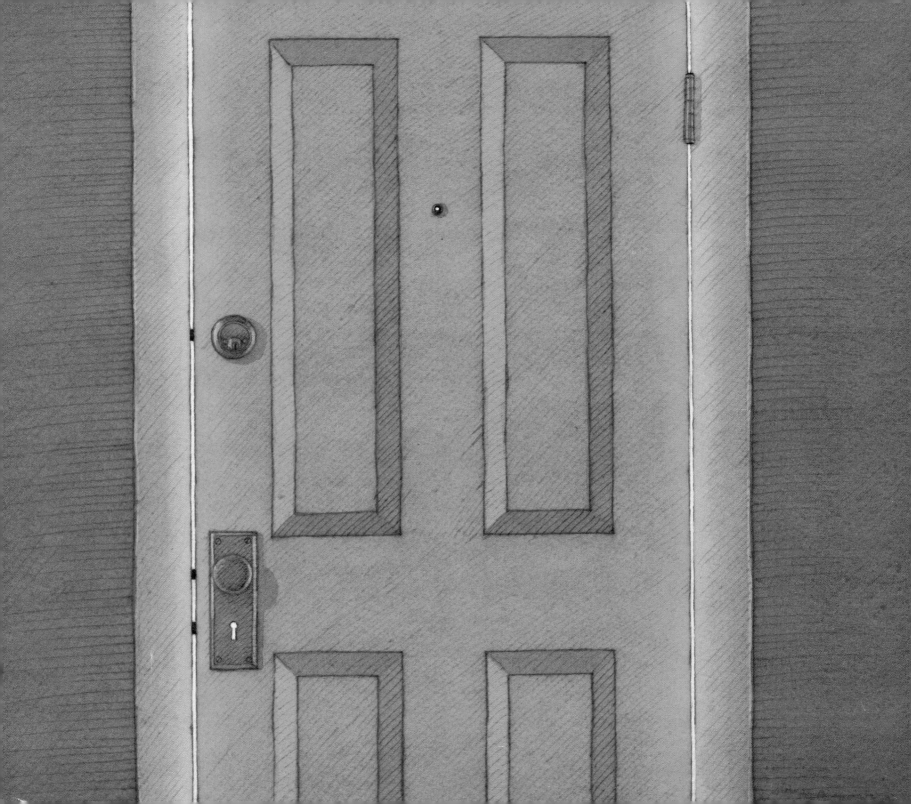

"Hi, Pizza Man!"

To the Mitnick kid

—V.W.

To my daughter, Emma

—P.G.

Orchard Books, 95 Madison Avenue, New York, NY 10016

Manufactured in the United States of America. Printed by Barton Press, Inc. Bound by Horowitz/Rae. Book design by Mina Greenstein. The text of this book is set in 16 pt. Futura Medium. The illustrations are ink line and acrylic wash reproduced in full color.
Hardcover 10 9 8 7 6 5 4 3 2
Paperback 10 9 8 7 6 5 4 3 2 1

Library of Congress Cataloging-in-Publication Data
Walter, Virginia. "Hi, pizza man!" / by Virginia Walter ; pictures by Ponder Goembel. p. cm. "A Richard Jackson book"—Half t.p.
Summary: While a young girl waits for the delivery of a hot pizza, she provides the appropriate animal sounds for a variety of pretend animal pizza deliverers.
ISBN 0-531-06885-4 (tr.) ISBN 0-531-08735-2 (lib. bdg.) ISBN 0-531-07107-3 (pbk.)
[1. Animal sounds—Fiction.] I. Goembel, Ponder, ill. II. Title. PZ7.W17126Hi 1995 [E]—dc20 94-24855